Cursed Journey
of the
Peculiar Bentleys

by Erin Palmer

Rourke
Educational Media
rourkeeducationalmedia.com

www.rourkeeducationalmedia.com

Edited by: Keli Sipperley
Cover and Interior layout by: Rhea Magaro
Cover Illustration by: Laura Tolton

Library of Congress PCN Data

Cursed Journey of the Peculiar Bentleys / Erin Palmer
 (History Files)
 ISBN (hard cover)(alk. paper) 978-1-68191-680-4
 ISBN (soft cover) 978-1-68191-781-8
 ISBN (e-Book) 978-1-68191-881-5
 Library of Congress Control Number: 2016932557

Printed in the United States of America,
North Mankato, Minnesota

Dear Parents and Teachers,

The History Files series takes readers into significant eras in United States history, allowing them to walk in the shoes of characters living in the periods they've learned about in the classroom. From the journey to a new beginning on the Mayflower, to the strife of the Vietnam War and beyond, each title in this series delves into the experiences of diverse characters struggling with the conflicts of their time.

Each book includes a comprehensive summary of the era, along with background information on the real people that the fictional characters mention or encounter in the novel. Additional websites to visit and an interview with the author are also included.

In addition, each title is supplemented with online teacher/parent notes with ideas for incorporating the book into a lesson plan. These notes include subject matter, background information, inspiration for maker space activities, comprehension questions, and additional online resources. Notes are available at: www.RourkeEducationalMedia.com.

We hope you enjoy the History Files books as much as we do.

Happy reading,
Rourke Educational Media

Table of Contents

Chapter One
A SPARK

Like many great adventures, the Bentley family's journey westward began with a spark. Well, two sparks, really.

There was the spark of imagination that grew in Robert Bentley from when he was a young boy. It was the sort of spark that made his insides feel itchy with the desire to travel. Robert wanted to learn; he wanted to meet new people and experience new things. That spark stayed with him as he moved into adulthood and became a husband and a father.

And then there was the actual spark: the one that ignited the Great Fire of Pittsburgh in 1845.

But for Robert's children, twins Eliza

and Leander Bentley, that was the day they confirmed what they always suspected: magic was real.

The morning of April 10, 1845, began in its usual way. As the sun rose over Pennsylvania, Eliza and Leander were busy with their morning chores. Eliza gathered the eggs from the hen house, milked Abigail, the family's sweet old cow, and then got down to her least favorite task: churning cream into butter.

To keep from going mad during the repetitive and boring work, Eliza would create her own songs. Instead of singing the typical churning songs that were common in her region, Eliza's lyrics were always much more personal and occasionally, if her mother was not in earshot, a bit mischievous.

"Poor Eliza, poor Eliza. Stuck with the silly butter churn. Leander is out in the world. When will it be Eliza's turn?" she sang with the up and down rhythm of the churning tub.

Many of her churning songs centered on how unfair it was that her twin had superior chores. As a boy, Leander's work took place outside and was much more varied than her own. Leander had to do physical jobs, like chopping wood, harvesting plants, and hunting. Eliza would have happily traded with him if it meant never having to cook another meal or darn another sock.

When the churning was done, Eliza figured there was time for a quick escape before she had to help prepare lunch. She wiped her hands on her apron and ran toward her favorite tree near the creek.

Leander was already there when she arrived, making shapes in the dirt with a stick. As usual, the twins seemed to have read each other's minds, something they were so used to doing, they barely noticed it anymore.

"New or old?" Leander asked without

looking up.

Eliza knew what he meant without further explanation. Leander made up the best games, but he would always let others choose if they should play something new or stick to a classic.

"New," Eliza said. "I have had more than enough of the same today with all that churning. Did you know that one in twelve girls die of churn-related boredom each day?"

They both laughed at the made-up fact. Their father was always saying "Did you know…" and following it up with some new and fascinating piece of information. He'd done this for as long as the twins could remember, filling their heads with facts, legends, and stories.

No one knew as much as their father, a man who loved learning so much, he would go without eating or sleeping when he got lost in a book. When the twins were four years old, Eliza climbed on top of the bench at church when everyone had their heads bent in prayer and shouted "Did you know that bunnies used to be BLUE?"

To this day, retelling that story delighted their father and made their mother flush with embarrassment. Making up silly new facts was a sure way to make her brother and father laugh, and making people laugh always made Eliza happy.

Before Leander could start shaping a new game, they heard Lucy Abbott, Eliza's best friend, shouting for her younger brothers.

"James and Noah Abbott, come out RIGHT NOW," Lucy yelled.

Lucy was always running after one brother or another, an unfortunate side effect of being the oldest of the six Abbott children. She feared the day when her baby sister would learn to walk. She especially feared the day when her sister would learn to run and hide, which seemed to be a favorite pastime of her brothers.

"Hi, Lucy," Leander called out. "Eliza and I were about to play a new game, it's too bad James and Noah aren't here to join us."

A nearby mulberry bush rustled. The two Abbott boys scrambled out from under it, insisting they wanted to play too.

The children gathered around Leander as he explained the rules to the new game. As usual, he made it up with ease and Eliza added an occasional imaginative detail.

Today's game was simple, as far as the twins' games went. For each round, someone would choose a color, then skip a rock across the creek. The number of times the rock bounced on the water before sinking would decide the number of items that the players had to find in the chosen color. Then the players would race back to the oak tree, with the first person back getting five points, the next four points and so on.

Since the creek was not very far across, the rock almost always skipped two or three times before sinking or reaching the opposite bank. Francis Bishop, the postman's son, swore that he was able to get a rock to skip four times last June, but no one was there to see it. When it was Lucy's turn to throw, it did not skip at all, leaving them to only find one item.

James and Noah, being the youngest and the most easily distracted of the bunch, did not do as well as the others. Lucy was good at finding things, but not a very fast runner, so she tended to be in the middle of the pack most rounds. Eliza and Leander were in fierce competition for first place when Leander added a twist and requested an item of two different colors.

"For this round, you have to find something

that is both pink and green," Leander said.

Eliza thought of the wildflowers that she picked on her way home from church on Sundays and took off running. Leander had the same thought and was half a step behind her in an instant. The Abbott boys, sick of losing each round, followed the twins. Lucy seemed to have another idea and set off toward the road that led to the marketplace where farmers, carpenters, and other artisans met each month to trade goods.

Though Leander reached the wildflowers first, Eliza managed to catch, then pass him. She reached the oak tree in record time, adding her flowers to the colorful pile of items they'd collected during the game so far, then used a stick to add five lines beneath her name in the dirt patch thcy were using to keep score.

After Leander, James, and Noah added their scores, they saw Lucy walking back toward them along the bank of the creek, staring down at something in her palm.

"Hurry up, slowpoke! You only get one point," Noah shouted.

Lucy didn't speed up. She didn't even look up. It was like she was watching a story unfold in her hand. Curiosity traveled through Eliza's whole body; it felt like a bubble formed at her toes and grew inside of her until it reached her head. She felt floaty and sure that if she didn't find out what her friend was holding right away, she would pop.

Her imagination raced as fast as her legs did as she ran over to Lucy. What in the world did her friend find?

When she was a few steps away, the mystery item looked like nothing more than a rock. But when she got closer, it was unlike any stone she'd ever seen.

It was about the size of Lucy's palm and

seemed to radiate every color at once. Shiny, black and slate-colored stones were not uncommon, but this was so much more than that. It was like holding a rainbow, but better. Because a rainbow's colors always stay in the same logical order, while this stone glistened with a shimmering iridescence that changed from blue to yellow to pink to green to purple and back again. It seemed to be all the colors and none of the colors at the same time, depending on how the sunlight hit it. Eliza opened her mouth to speak, but couldn't find the right words to compliment such a magnificent item.

The boys ambled over to see what had Lucy and Eliza so captivated. When they saw the stone, they too were struck silent. The five of them just stared quietly at Lucy's palm, surely breaking a record for their longest stretch of silence while playing together.

"What is it?" Noah eventually asked.

"A rock or mineral, I guess," Lucy said.

"That's no ordinary rock," Eliza said, confirming out loud what they were all thinking.

She reached out and ran her fingers over the nooks and crevices. Just touching the stone sent a surge of excitement through her. In that moment, everything from her muddy shoes to the cloudy skies seemed to be more beautiful than they ever had before.

"It was in the grass near the road to Pittsburgh," Lucy said. "I was going to pick one of those berries near the Miller's farm, but I saw this sparkling as I ran by. I wonder if some sort of merchant dropped it on his way to trade."

"I want to hold it! Give it to me," James said, reaching for the stone.

"No, me! I want to see it," Noah said.

Lucy shrieked as her brothers grabbed the

stone from her, fighting each other to try to rip it from the other one's hand.

"Be careful," Leander said, grabbing Noah's arm and pulling him away from his brother.

"Don't lose it," Eliza said at almost the same moment, wrapping her arms around James (in a most unladylike manner that would horrify her mother) and pulling him away.

The combined force of all the pushing, pulling, and poking sent the stone flying into the air toward the creek. The five of them drew a collected breath in panic, because they knew the precious stone was about to drop into the water and likely be lost forever.

But that is not what happened.

Instead of sinking, the stone skipped. That was extraordinary enough, as it was way too misshapen and lumpy to make for a good skipping stone. But the really incredible thing was how it skipped. Not twice or three times, like most stones. Not four times like the unconfirmed stone that Francis Bishop loved to boast about. Not even five times, which would have been an unheard of record in their town.

Somehow, the stone skipped seven times, an impossible feat given the width of the creek. It bounced up and down in narrow arches, getting way more height than any rock could tangibly achieve without sinking. With the sparkling colors and unimaginable motions, it looked more like a fairy diving in and out of the water than a stone that slipped out of a scuffle.

The whole thing happened so fast; *plip, plip, plip, plip, plip, plip, plip,* it splashed across the water and landed on the other side of the creek. The very air seemed hazy and the smell of burned earth wafted through the wind.

"Magic," Noah whispered.

Without thinking, Eliza plunged into the creek. Though her mother would be furious at the state of her, this was far too important to worry about proper behavior. She grabbed the stone with great care and trudged back through the water. As much as she loved the feel of it, she returned it to Lucy. It was only fair.

The very moment the stone left her hand, she heard a man shouting, then another. Soon shouting adult voices seemed to come from everywhere at once, so many that it was hard to distinguish one from the next. Eliza could not make out a word of it.

Mr. Amos Grissom went rushing by, heading toward the Miller farm as fast as his old legs could carry him, which was not all that fast. In his haste, he did not notice the children until Leander startled him by calling out.

"Mr. Grissom, what's going on, sir?"

"You kids better run home, now! It's the end of days, I tell ya," Mr. Grissom said, wiping his forehead with a handkerchief. "It's burning up, every last bit of it! The entire city of Pittsburgh is on fire!"

Chapter Two
A CHANGE IN LUCK

News of the fire spread as fast as the fire itself. Since the Bentley family's farm was just outside of Pittsburgh, Robert and many of the other men in town rushed off to see if they could help.

Phoebe Bentley, Eliza and Leander's mother, was busy making lunch when the twins got home. She calmly told the children where their father went and asked them to wash up for lunch.

"But will Father be safe? Mr. Grissom said it was the end of days," Eliza said.

"Nonsense," her mother replied. "You know your father, he is smart enough to stay safe.

But he may not be home until late, I expect he'll be the last one over there, helping as many as he can."

Leander seemed satisfied with that explanation and sat down to eat. Though their mother seemed as calm as always, Eliza knew better. She saw the way her mother's foot was tapping beneath the table. She noticed that her mother, like herself, could not stomach more than a few bites of lunch.

Eliza's own stomach was full of anxiety. Her friend Lucy always called it nervous butterflies in the stomach, but to Eliza it felt more like nervous grasshoppers leaping about inside her.

But the real reason why Eliza knew her mother was nervous was that she always scolded Eliza for coming home late, filthy and soaking wet. Eliza's brown curls had escaped from her bonnet. The same woman who could notice a miniscule speck on

Eliza's apron from across the room did not even seem to notice that her daughter was a total mess. Eliza felt certain this was the sign of something terrible.

Later that night, as Leander slept peacefully, Eliza lay very still in her bed, listening for the return of her father. She could not sleep until she knew that he was safe at home. Though the house was silent, Eliza knew that her mother was awake as well, probably with the feeling of nervous grasshoppers in her stomach to match Eliza's. Or maybe everyone's nerves felt different, Eliza thought. Her mother might have nervous hummingbirds flying in her stomach or nervous trout swimming in there. Eliza felt like she had to know what her mother was feeling right in that moment, so she crawled out of bed.

Just as she expected, her mother was sitting in the dark at the kitchen table.

Phoebe's straight blonde hair was neatly

tucked into her sleep bonnet. Her wide brown eyes were staring straight ahead. She looked calm as always, but Eliza could see her toes tapping under the table.

"Mother," Eliza whispered so she wouldn't wake Leander. "What animal does it feel like is in your belly when you're nervous?"

If Phoebe was startled, she didn't show it. She lit a candle to better see her daughter, and though she wanted to send the girl to bed, Eliza's troubled expression was too much to bear as she chattered more about stomachs, butterflies, and grasshoppers.

"What do you mean? You know there are no animals in our stomachs," Phoebe said.

"Butterflies in stomach is an idiom, Mother," Eliza said. "Father says that idioms are phrases that are used in a figurative way to express something different from the actual meaning."

Phoebe sighed and wondered, not for the

first time, if her children were too smart for their own good. Especially Eliza. Though she was proud of the twins, she worried about them too. Especially her daughter.

Phoebe thought back on a recent morning after church, when her husband was talking to the postman about some poem about a raven. Leander was teaching all four of the wild Abbott boys a game of some sort and Eliza, that bold girl, was asking the pastor question after question about the Bible. Just as Eliza asked if the disciples ever told each other jokes, Phoebe heard one of the parishioners whispering about their family.

"Those Bentleys are just so peculiar."

Phoebe did not turn to see who it was. It didn't matter. She knew that their neighbors respected them. Robert was always the first to help others and the family worked harder than anyone. Robert was a sometimes carpenter, sometimes farmer. He could earn far more if he focused on carpentry, as he was the most talented carpenter for miles. But he only liked to work on a piece if the wood "spoke to him."

There was no question that her imaginative husband was indeed peculiar, and passed on many of these traits to their children. He was always telling them stories and teaching them things, sometimes things they probably shouldn't know. The three of them had so much imagination. Robert was a deep thinker, but he was always quick to laugh. He and the twins laughed all the time, and if they noticed the strange looks from neighbors, they didn't care.

Phoebe herself was abundantly normal in every way but one: she loved her peculiar husband and children with all of her heart.

She was thinking of this when Robert finally arrived home from Pittsburgh. Eliza cried out with joy and flung herself into her father's arms, knocking over her chair in the process. Though part of Phoebe wanted to do the same thing, she calmly straightened Eliza's chair before rising to meet her husband. She wrapped her arms around her husband and daughter both, breathing in the scent of fire that clung to her husband's beard.

"It seems most of the people are safe," Robert said. "But the devastation! Thousands of buildings and homes destroyed in an instant. The Bank of Pittsburgh, the mayor's office, churches, all gone."

Robert took a deep breath and stared off into space. Eliza looked up at her father, feeling the grasshoppers starting to hop again. Her father's blue-green eyes, which always looked like they were smiling, had taken on a serious expression Eliza had never seen. He looked at her mother and before he even opened his mouth, Eliza knew his next words would change their lives.

"Phoebe, everything ends in time. There is so much more to see, to do," he said quietly. "I think we should go west."

Though Eliza was sent off to bed, she knew her parents talked long into the night. In the weeks that followed, she often caught them in deep discussion. As a man, her father could just make the decision alone, but he valued his wife and did not want to command her into such a serious decision. It was after her father read aloud an article about Manifest Destiny, and how it was God's desire for America to grow, that her mother decided perhaps the move was the right thing to do.

So they began preparations. Throughout the summer, then autumn when the twins turned thirteen, and through the holidays, the family readied for the pending journey. While they rang in 1846, their last New Year's Day in Pennsylvania, they prepared. Every moment of every day was busy gathering supplies and planning for the move, which would begin that spring.

During this time, Eliza was struggling with a streak of bad luck that would not relent. It started when she spilled a week's worth of milk, putting the family behind in their butter and cheese production. To have enough money and supplies for the trip, Robert was focusing on some big carpentry pieces, which meant keeping the schedule for the farm work was even more crucial than ever. They brought in good money with their dairy products, so a spill was costly. Though her mother was kind about it, Eliza felt guilty. Then it happened again, another week's work gone in a stumble. This time her mother told her she had to be more careful. After the third incident, Eliza really started to worry.

That wasn't all. It seemed every day brought a new problem. She dropped eggs. She accidently stepped on their dog, Poe, who ran in front of a passing horse, who bucked and threw their neighbor off its back. No one was hurt, but it was distressing all the same. She ripped a hole in her holiday dress when it caught on a bramble on the way to church because she was picking flowers instead of paying attention to her clothes. From small things to big ones, Eliza became a walking disaster. The nervous grasshoppers jumped in her stomach almost every single day.

The day before the Bentleys were due to leave, Eliza and Lucy planned to meet at their favorite tree one last time. Eliza got there first, and though she knew her mother would be furious if she found out, she pulled up her dress and climbed the tree. It was a perfect spring day, and Eliza tried to take in the view of the creek, the feel of the tree and the smell of the wildflowers for the final time. But she had a lot of feelings. Too many feelings. Confusing feelings.

She was thrilled for the chance to see so many new things. She was curious at what her new life would be like once they got to Oregon. But she was also scared. Not just of the journey, but of an awful idea that had been growing inside of her for months. If Manifest Destiny was God telling Americans to grow and expand, did that mean her recent bad luck was a sign of destiny too?

Her heart pounded thinking about how much trouble a cursed girl could cause on such a perilous journey. They had about a half a year of travel ahead of them, with plenty of danger along the way. Should she even go if she was only going to bring bad luck to her family and all of the other travelers? But if she stayed behind, she would only bring bad luck to her friends here in town. Where could she go to keep the world safe from her?

"Eliza," Lucy called out from the ground below. "I've been calling for you, did you not hear me?"

In her hectic climb down the tree, Eliza lost her footing and accidently kicked Lucy right in the chin.

"Oh no, oh no," Eliza said. "Are you hurt?"

She wanted to examine Lucy for injuries, but she was afraid to get any closer. This was a sure sign that she was indeed cursed. Eliza burst into tears.

"Eliza, I am fine," Lucy said. "Please don't cry! What is wrong?"

Eliza plopped down in the grass, sobbing, oblivious to such things as dirt and proper posture. Lucy sat primly next to her, keeping her skirt neatly arranged and her back straight as Eliza's worried words tumbled from her lips.

By the time she was done explaining, Eliza had stopped crying. Lucy pulled a pristine lace handkerchief out of her apron and began wiping Eliza's tear-and-dirt-streaked face.

"Oh, I will miss your imagination so," Lucy said. "I do not think you are cursed at all, it is probably just nerves about the journey."

"No, it is more than that," Eliza said. "I can feel it!"

"Well then," Lucy said in the same problem-solver voice she used when helping her brothers. "Just to be safe, we will have to make sure you are protected with some good luck."

Lucy reached into her apron again and pulled out the beautiful stone they found the day of the fire. The stone that seemed to be magical. Eliza's eyes grew wide as Lucy handed the stone to her.

"Oh, Lucy, I couldn't! It is so beautiful and it might be valuable."

"I want you to have it, Eliza," Lucy said. "Consider it a token of our friendship, so you will never forget me."

A quiet moment passed as each girl realized that after a lifetime of friendship, this might be the last time they ever saw each other. Tears welled up in each girl's eyes. Eliza hugged Lucy tightly. Lucy hugged Eliza tightly right back. Their tears flowed freely until Lucy pulled two more spotless handkerchiefs out of her apron. This struck Eliza as hysterical. She erupted in giggles. Those giggles were contagious; Lucy caught them, too.

"How many more of these do you have in there?" Eliza wiped Lucy's face as Lucy wiped hers, which further fueled their laughter.

"With my brothers, there are not enough clean handkerchiefs in the world," Lucy said. "Do you feel any better now that you have a good luck charm?"

"Though the stone is lovely, how do we know it would even bring luck?" Eliza asked, solemn again.

"Didn't you say you felt something special when you held it?" Lucy asked.

Eliza nodded, but she looked skeptical.

"I have proof that it is a lucky stone," Lucy said. "With all of your travel preparations, I forgot to tell you, the Smith family is moving! A relative left them some land in Virginia, so they are going to be gone for good!"

The Smith family were the Abbotts' neighbors; their families' farms were right next to each other. Lucy's parents considered Phillip Smith, the oldest son, a good potential future husband for Lucy. Their union would create one of the largest farms in the region. This always distressed and disgusted Lucy and Eliza. Phillip was the sort of boy who kicked cats and always seemed to have a runny nose.

"That is wonderful news," Eliza said. "I can leave in peace knowing that you will not have to wipe snot off your face after your wedding kiss. Though Lord knows you'd probably have enough handkerchiefs for the job!"

The friends started giggling again. With the lucky stone in her hand, sitting by her favorite tree with her best friend, Eliza felt lighter and happier than she had in months. The curse seemed to be broken at last.

Chapter Three
CURSED ON THE TRAIL

Some of the goodbyes were harder than others. Eliza had no trouble when her father traded away the chickens, with their clucking, pecking, and endless egg laying. But she was furious to learn that sweet Abigail, the cow that she spent so many hours with, was too old to make the journey. Luckily, Robert traded Abigail to Lucy's father in exchange for some flour, biscuits, and other supplies. Lucy promised Eliza she would take special care of Abigail.

Lucy, of course, was Eliza's saddest goodbye. After hugging, crying and promising to write, Eliza did one final favor for her dearest friend. She gathered Lucy's brothers, bent down until she was eye-level with them and spoke to them in a voice that was both quiet and menacing.

"Have you ever heard of the wild twin spirits that haunt the Oregon Trail?" she asked. The boys shook their heads. "Well, legend says that these wild spirits will attack any unruly children they come across."

"And they can only be controlled by other twins," Leander said, picking up the story even though Eliza was making it up as she went along. "So Eliza and I can send them after any unruly children we choose."

"Lucy will write me with updates of your behavior," Eliza said. "So you better listen to your sister ... or else."

The next morning at dawn, the Bentleys and three other local families set out on their way to Independence, Missouri, where they would meet up with hundreds of other travelers to make their way to the Oregon Trail.

Their wagons were full to the brim with hundreds of pounds of flour, bacon, salt, sugar, and lard. There was cornmeal, dried beans, molasses, coffee, baking soda, dried fruit, and dried beef. They had clothes, bedding, tents and all kinds of tools. These were the same sort of supplies that all of the travelers brought, but of course, the Bentleys were not quite the same as the other travelers; a good portion of their second wagon held Robert's massive collection of books.

Phoebe was not keen on this idea, and she tried her hardest to convince Robert to leave them behind, or at least some of them.

"I'd sooner leave behind Leander," Robert had replied with a wink, making the twins laugh. "A life without books would be like spending eternity stuck in one place without moving a step. I intend to travel as far as the words will take me."

So that was that. With the supplies and the books taking up so much space in the wagons, there was not much space for sitting, so the family walked along the wagons for the twelve day journey to Independence. From the very start, the family was blessed with the sort of luck that made Eliza feel like the lucky stone was working.

First, there was the weather. It was early May and it looked like storms could roll in at any minute. They could see the storm clouds in the distance, but not once did they suffer through one. It was as if the storms were traveling at the same pace that they were, always in the distance, but just out of reach.

There was also the matter of the new cow. Several of the families from town chipped in to purchase the cow, with the agreement that they would all take care of her and share her dairy. Eliza disliked the cow from the start, as it was moody and squirmy while being milked, nothing like Abigail. Eliza had taken to calling the cow Anti-Abigail and felt sure that she would waste many precious hours of the trip trying to get the creature to cooperate.

But to her immense joy, the parents of seven-year-old Emma Miller insisted that their daughter do the milking; they wanted her to get used to the task before they reached Independence. Eliza kissed her stone when she heard the news.

At night, the family gathered around the fire, with Poe curled at their feet sleeping and occasionally chasing after small animals, proudly bringing back rabbits every so often. Though they had tents, when the weather was especially nice, Eliza and Leander would join their father and sleep directly under the stars.

On one such night, as her brother and father snored quietly beside her and her mother slept peacefully in a tent, Eliza felt a well of pent-up energy inside of her. All of the miles she walked and those still ahead made her feel full of life in a way that she never knew was possible. She felt like if she jumped in the air, she would take off and fly. Poe seemed to be excited too. He trotted over and dropped a knotted piece of rope at her feet.

"Want to play?" Eliza whispered.

Poe wagged his tail and ran in a circle. Eliza stood up quietly, careful not wake up her family, and walked away from the campsites. The moon was full and bright in the sky; even in the dark, she could see a clear spot with space to play.

She threw the rope as far as she could, then ran after it herself as if she were racing her pup. Of course, Poe reached the rope first each time. Still, it felt wonderful to run full-speed in the quiet night.

As she ran past a small clump of trees, Eliza wondered how many types of trees there were in the world and how many she would get to see during her lifetime. Her musings were interrupted when her foot slipped on a rock. "Oomph," she grunted as she hit the ground. Poe came running back. He backed up toward her and sat on her lap. Eliza giggled.

Then Poe stood up. The fur on his back bristled as he unfurled a deep growl. His body stiffened; his ears pointed straight up. Eliza's stomach churned. They'd run far from camp. Whatever Poe was growling at, there was no one around to help. She stayed still, her eyes sweeping the woods for something out of the ordinary.

Then, she saw it.

The wolf was so massive, it hardly looked real. It bared its teeth, its eyes staring directly at Eliza like she was all there was in the world. She had never been looked at like that, with such intensity and terrifying purpose. Her fear was paralyzing. She wasn't sure if she was breathing.

The wolf moved slowly toward her. Poe was between them, growling and showing his teeth. As the animals moved closer to one another, something flew through the sky, fast and silent, and struck the wolf.

A lot of things happened at once in that moment. The wolf dropped with a thud. Poe stopped moving and looked to the left, where the mystery flying object came from. Eliza saw a man standing there, holding a bow. A boy, probably about her age, stood beside him, with a bow and arrow pointed at the wolf, in case it should get up. Poe growled again, unsure what to make of the strangers. Then something else caught the dog's attention. A small light, seemingly suspended in mid-air, quickly floated toward them. Poe ran toward it, and as it got closer, Eliza saw that it was her father, holding a lantern and a rifle, running her way with Poe at his heels.

Robert dropped to his knees when he reached Eliza. He wrapped his arms around her. Her face was wet against his neck. It was only then she realized she was crying.

"Stay here with Poe," Robert said, putting the lantern down and raising his hand at the dog in a gesture that meant "stay."

Eliza didn't want her father to leave, but she didn't think she could stand if she tried. She wrapped her arms around Poe as her father made his way toward the two natives.

The younger one was no longer aiming his bow, but the older one reached back and grabbed an arrow. Robert paused, keeping eye contact, and placed his gun on the ground.

"I won't hurt you," he said, raising his hands. "Do you understand?"

The younger one said something Eliza didn't understand. The older man nodded, but kept the arrow in his hand.

"He speaks no English," the boy said.

"And he does not trust your people."

"I understand," Robert said. "I am sure you have faced a lot. But please let him know that he just saved my daughter's life and I will forever be grateful."

The boy spoke again. The man lowered his bow.

"We are making our way to Independence, then following the Oregon Trail," Robert said.

"My father and I are too," the boy said.

"You are welcome to join our group," Robert said.

Eliza did not understand what the boy said to his father, but the man shook his head at once.

"If you ever need anything, my name is Robert. Travel safe, gentlemen," Robert said. "And thank you."

The boy translated to his father. The man looked Robert in the eyes and gave a single nod.

Robert picked up his gun and made his way back to Eliza. Though she was thirteen years old, her father scooped her up like she was a small child and walked back to camp, Poe following behind them. She saw the boy and his father make their way to the fallen wolf, and she buried her face in her father's neck to avoid seeing what would happen next.

The family woke the next morning when the sky opened up, dumping sheets of sharp rain on the camp. The downpour felt like a bad omen to Eliza. She reached in her apron pocket for her lucky stone.

It wasn't there.

She pulled off her shoes, checked her socks, and checked under her bonnet. The stone was gone. She must have lost it running with Poe the night before. That would explain the incident with the wolf, she thought. Her luck had turned again.

Eliza felt cold to her core. Part of that was due to her bare feet and the pouring rain, but it was mostly because she could feel the luck draining from her.

"Eliza! Get dressed, we have to start moving," her mother said. "We should get to Independence by nightfall, but it is going to be a lot harder in this rain."

Her father pulled her aside after the family ate a quick breakfast of biscuits and jam. He spoke to her in a tone she was unfamiliar with; one that sounded like he was talking to another adult. An adult who was precious to him.

"You cannot run off like that, my girl," Robert said. "I understand why you did. I feel it too, very often, that pull toward the unknown and desire to follow my whims. I wish we lived in a world where you could wander wherever and whenever you want. But there are dangers."

He looked at his daughter, her brown curls refusing to be contained by her bonnet. She had his wild hair and blue-green eyes; wide, like her mother's. Those eyes always made it easy to see just how Eliza felt. And, right now, those eyes looked troubled.

"That doesn't mean you should be afraid, Eliza," Robert said. "A life controlled by fear is not one lived to the fullest. You just have to learn how to be adventurous and aware at the same time."

He patted his daughter's cheek. Though Eliza felt slightly warmed by her father's words, she still felt worried. The sky stayed dark, the rain kept pounding on them, and the road got muddier and muddier.

One of their wagon wheels got stuck in the mud and it took almost an hour to get it loose. Eliza and Leander were struggling to lift their feet out of the mud with each step. When it got to the point where they were sinking into the mud to their ankles, Robert stopped the wagon.

He pulled out some of his books and wrapped them in a burlap sack, clearing space so Eliza and Leander could sit in the wagon. Watching her father tuck some of his beloved books into the nook of a tree, Eliza felt both loved and guilty. It couldn't be a coincidence that the family faced such bad luck from the moment she lost her stone.

"I'm sorry about your books," Eliza said when her father came back to the wagon and helped her and Leander into the small space.

"No apologies necessary. I was lucky to read them and hopefully a future traveler will see them in that tree and get to experience that joy," Robert said, smiling.

As they continued on their way, Eliza put her head on Leander's shoulder. Within minutes, Leander cried out and rubbed his arm, just under where Eliza's head was resting moments before. He had been bitten by a spider. A purplish patch had already began to spread on his arm.

Their mother examined the wound and assured the fretful Eliza that the spider was not poisonous. Eliza didn't have the heart to admit to her family that it wasn't the spider she was worried about. She was the poison.

Chapter Four
FROM BAD TO WORSE

Even with the rain, the group managed to make it to Independence in decent time. When the rain finally stopped, Eliza and Leander peeked out of the wagon. Hundreds of other travelers were there making camp for the night. There was something so beautiful about seeing people from different parts of the country meeting in one spot, all on their own journeys, but together all the same. Eliza almost forgot about the curse until her mother called out for her to milk the cow.

"I thought little Emma was milking these days," Eliza said.

"Well Emma is exhausted from the walk

and you have been riding in a wagon," Phoebe said. "We all do our parts around here."

Of course, milking Anti-Abigail took ages, so Eliza didn't have time to check out the campsite or meet any of the other travelers before nightfall. The bad luck continued when she made her way to where her family was gathered around the fire and saw the butter churn waiting for her.

Her father was wringing out his boots, trying to get them dry before the next day's journey. Her mother was darning socks and Leander was playing his fiddle. Normally Eliza would feel frustrated churning butter while Leander was free of chores, but his music was the loveliest part of the evening.

The calm did not last long. Shouts erupted from one of the other travelers, a giant of a man with one of the largest beards Eliza had ever seen.

"Men, follow me! We will not let these

savages anywhere near our families," the man yelled.

Robert stood and rushed over to the man without stopping to put on his boots first. He stood there in his muddy socks and tried to calm the man down. After a few minutes of discussion, it became clear that the large man was trying to gather a group together to attack some natives. A few minutes of further discussion revealed the targets were the man and boy who saved Eliza from the wolf.

"Those men are of no danger to us," Robert said.

"No danger?" the man bellowed, gathering attention from everyone around him. "They are *savages*. We must attack them before they attack us."

"The only savage behavior I see is from you, to be honest," Robert said, keeping his voice calm. "That man and his boy saved my daughter's life. I repeat, those men are no danger to us."

The crowd seemed to calm down, but the large man was unmoved.

"What about Manifest Destiny?" the man shouted. "It is God's will for us to take this land. Who are you to argue that?"

"I am not arguing against Manifest Destiny," Robert said, stepping forward and putting his arm on the man's shoulder. "But God's will is not meant to harm innocent families who already live on this land. It is about expansion, but that does not have to mean conquering. Do we really want to start this new life with unnecessary violence and bloodshed?"

It seemed like the man might punch Robert in the face. Eliza could see he was unconvinced by her father's words. He clenched his fists and jaw, narrowing his eyes as he stared at Robert, sizing him up. Then he shook off Robert's arm and stormed away.

Though there was no angry mob running

off to attack anyone, Eliza could see that her father's speech did not crush the violence in many of the men's eyes. It was heartbreaking for her to realize that the beauty she felt earlier about people from all over coming together for one journey did not include all people.

Many of these travelers only wanted to be surrounded by people who looked like them, thought like them, and shared the same narrow view of the world. Since her family was so different, would they ever find a place where they belonged? And even if such a place existed, would they even make it there with this curse hanging over them?

Travel began at first light the next morning. Just before dawn, when almost everyone was still asleep, Eliza heard her father gathering some supplies and heading out of camp. When he returned, he had his arms full of animal pelts. Eliza knew he had been trading with the Indians.

The ground was still muddy, but with the new pelts and some fresh game, the wagon no longer had space for Leander and Eliza.

"So no real rules for this one," Leander said as they walked beside the wagon. "Whenever someone passes, we will take turns guessing what their lives are like."

"That family is full of circus performers," Eliza said. "As soon as we all go to sleep at night, they untether their oxen and practice the most daring acts the world has ever seen. Because they feel that horses are overrated and showy."

"We actually love horses," a girl's voice said from behind them. "But your version of our lives is far more interesting than the truth."

The girl, a member of the group that had just passed, straggled behind her family, preferring to keep her own pace. Leander explained the game to her and she laughed.

"My name is Harriet Mathers, what are your names?"

"I'm Eliza and he's Leander," Eliza said.

"Leander and Eliza Bentley," Leander said at the same time.

"Oh, *you're* the Bentleys," Harriet said. "Your family is the talk of the trail! Such ideas you have. May I walk with you?"

Eliza had her guard up, worried about letting a new person into her cursed life. But as the day went on, she started to enjoy the first steps toward friendship. Harriet was fascinated by their family without being judgemental. She also had a tendency to say whatever she was thinking.

"You aren't as strange as I expected," Harriet said. "You are strange, but in a wonderful way."

Eliza laughed and at that exact moment, Harriet cried out. Her foot got caught in the mud and she twisted her ankle. Phoebe and Robert came over and helped Harriet get free.

As they wrapped up her ankle and helped her back to her family, Eliza and Leander sat near the wagon and watched a worm slither through the mud. It seemed like hard work for the little worm to move just a few feet. Just as it finally reached a patch of grass, a bird swooped down and ate it.

"Isn't it crazy how even when it seems like nothing is happening, life and death are going on all around us?" Leander asked, before walking away to get the oxen ready to start moving again.

Eliza just sat there, marveling at her brother's ability to say something so profound and not even notice. She also wondered how her twin, who always seemed to be able to read her mind, could be so oblivious to her curse. She wanted to tell him, but worried that speaking it out loud would make matters even worse.

Things continued to go wrong as the trip

continued. Two of their oxen died and they lost time and money replacing them. When the family unloaded their wagons after they ferried across the Missouri River, they realized that some of their supplies had been stolen.

After walking all day, Robert had to work late into the night on his carpentry by firelight to try to earn money to replace the lost supplies. He was so exhausted that one night he nodded off by the fire and singed his eyebrows.

Eliza never understood the purpose of eyebrows until she saw her father without them. Eyebrows seem to exist to keep people from looking totally crazy.

Even though Eliza tried to stay away, Harriet insisted on spending time with the Bentleys. It should have been easy to stay away from a girl with a sprained ankle, but Harriet got her family to travel right in front of the Bentleys, so she could talk to Eliza and Leander from the back of her family's wagon. When it was time to do chores, Harriet would prop her foot up on a stool that Robert made for her and churn butter, sew clothes, or milk cows right alongside Eliza.

Despite herself, Eliza became fond of Harriet and the entire Mathers family. Mr. Mathers was quiet, but played harmonica so beautifully that it cut straight into Eliza's soul. Mrs. Mathers was always the first to laugh at a joke and she had a very soothing way with animals, even Anti-Abigail. And Harriet's three littles sisters, all under the age of five, were adorable and amusing.

Eliza couldn't help but laugh whenever little Cora would toddle after Leander, bombarding him with questions.

"Leander, why is the moon a moon?" she asked him one evening as the children sat around the fire with Phoebe, preparing supper.

Before Leander could answer, Robert returned from a hunt, and pulled Phoebe aside to talk to her. Harriet's parents were off near their own wagon, which was much further away than usual.

To Eliza's horror, her calm mother looked panicked and her eyes filled with tears. Robert wiped his wife's tears away and kissed her forehead before making his way to the children.

"We would be honored if the Mathers ladies would make camp with us this evening," Robert said.

Harriet and her sisters were excited, but Eliza could tell something was wrong. When her father went to gather more firewood, Eliza took off after him and demanded answers.

"Mrs. Mathers has dysentery," Robert said, removing his hat and looking down at his boots. "She is very ill and her husband thought it best to keep the girls away, just in case."

Eliza spent the rest of the night and the following morning feeling empty in her chest but busy in her mind. She didn't know what to do, what to say, or how she was meant to behave.

Mr. Mathers pulled his daughters aside later that morning to tell them that their mother was too ill to travel that day. They decided to stay put another day in hopes that Mrs. Mathers would recover. Robert and Phoebe, despite being on such a tight schedule, stayed with them to help watch over the children while Mr. Mathers tended to his wife.

Though the kids had spent weeks wishing for a day off from traveling, they were unsure how to proceed. Even little Cora was quiet most of the day. At twilight, Mr. Mathers made his way back to the group, his hat in hand, staring at the ground. He looked up at his daughters, opened his mouth to speak, then shut it again.

Harriet started sobbing before her father could say the words she knew were coming.

"She's gone," Mr. Mathers said. "Your mother is with the angels now."

Phoebe gathered Harriet in her arms as the girl cried with her entire body. Though the younger girls did not quite understand what was happening, they started crying too. Phoebe pulled them into the hug and said soft, soothing words. She remained like that for over an hour until the girls eventually fell into an exhausted sleep.

The following day was painful for everyone. Mrs. Mathers was buried on the side of the road. Robert dug the grave, choosing a spot beneath a beautiful tree. There was barely time for a prayer before Mr. Mathers loaded his girls into their wagon and headed off in the opposite direction. Losing his wife left him shaken and he decided he couldn't bear traveling on for months into an unknown future.

He thanked Robert and Phoebe for their kindness and headed back to Boston, where he still had family. Harriet waved sadly at Eliza and Leander from the back of her wagon until it was out of sight.

Eliza was barely able to sleep after Mrs. Mathers died. She tossed and turned, plagued by nightmares about curses and disease. One night, she awoke screaming. Her mother crawled into her tent and held her until she fell back asleep. When she awoke again, she heard someone retching outside of the tent.

She turned to ask her mother who it was, but Phoebe was gone. The nervous grasshoppers returned to Eliza's stomach as she peeked out of the tent and confirmed what she feared: her mother was gravely ill.

Chapter Five
REVELATIONS

Eliza tried to convince herself that it was a coincidence. Her mother would be fine; she had to be. It must have been a fluke. But as the travel continued, Phoebe continued to get sick almost every day. She tried to hide it, but Eliza was watching her closely.

Illness seemed to tear through the travelers. Tainted drinking water led to an outbreak of cholera. As the Bentley family reached Wyoming, they saw many makeshift graves on the side of the road. Occasionally bodies were simply left behind. Robert always stopped and dug a quick grave for the deceased stranger, even when he was exhausted by the travel and the stifling heat.

Though their spirits were low, they tried to perk up as they neared Independence Rock. Despite the unplanned stops during their journey, they managed to time it so they would reach Independence Rock by the Fourth of July. There would be a big Independence Day celebration and they were going to carve their names in the rock like so many travelers before them.

Leander was excited about the celebration and tried to get Eliza excited too.

"I have a new game idea," he said when the family was a few miles from Independence Rock.

"Not now, Leander," Eliza said.

"Why not? You're being weird," Leander said. "Even for you."

Eliza laughed. She was about to tell him everything: her worries, the curse, and their mother's secret illness. But before she could say anything, she heard her mother gasp.

"Look away, children," Robert said.

But it was too late. Eliza saw the body. It was an Indian man, very old, with very long white hair. Based on his age, she would have assumed that he died a natural death, but the blood all over his clothes made it obvious his death was a violent one.

Robert stopped the family's wagons and started digging a grave. Phoebe took a quilt she had spent the past week making and draped it over the man. When the grave was finished, Leander helped his father lower the body into the ground.

Just as Robert finished covering the grave with the last shovelful of dirt, a wagon stopped beside them.

"You should be disgusted with yourself," a man called out. He was tall and thin, with a very angry face. "It is Independence Day and here you are mucking about with the body of savage."

The man spit toward the grave and hurried his wagon along.

"Father, why do our people hate the native people so much?" Leander asked.

"Robert," Phoebe began, trying to end the conversation.

"No, Phoebe, it's fine," Robert said. "I want my children to have inquiring minds and opinions of their own, no matter how strange that may be to others."

As the family found a place to camp for the night and started getting their tents up and doing their chores, Robert explained to his children how settlers have impacted the lives of the native people.

"Imagine if one day, strange people showed up at our doorstep and said our house was theirs," Robert said. "And imagine we stood our ground to try to keep our home and the strangers started attacking. What do you think would happen?"

"More fighting?" Eliza guessed.

"Exactly," Robert said. "Our people were the strangers. The Indians lived here first, and we disrupted that life. Yes, they sometimes attacked us. We sometimes attacked them as well. Many lives have been lost."

"Is that what happened to the old man we just buried?" Leander asked.

"I can't know for certain, but I think it is very likely," Robert said.

"But he was so old," Leander said. "Why would anyone hurt someone who poses no threat?"

"Some people are threatened by what they don't understand," Robert explained. "That is why I make sure to read and learn. I feel it helps make the world less confusing when you have a wider perspective."

"And that man who just spit, I guess he has not read much?" Leander asked.

Robert laughed loudly, the sound bursting like the boom of a cannon.

"You are likely right, son," Robert said. "People who do not take the time to learn new things and challenge existing ideas are often doomed to repeat the same mistakes. Many believe they have to rule and conquer lands in order to enjoy them. As a pacifist, I do not believe that violence and bloodshed are necessarily the best way to build a future. There is enough sickness and danger in the world without adding to it."

Robert and Phoebe looked at each other. Eliza started thinking about how ill her mother was. She turned her head so her family would not see her tears, but she wasn't quick enough.

"Robert, please, you are upsetting Eliza," Phoebe said.

Eliza's hands were hidden beneath the new quilt that she was working on with her mother, since they buried their last one. She gave herself a little jab with the sewing needle, and held up her finger to show her parents.

"Not at all," Eliza said. "My needle just slipped a bit."

She could not tell them that she was the reason the old man had died. She was the reason that her mother was sick. The bad luck was like a storm cloud, following her every step.

"Well, I would love to carve my name in a very large rock right about now," Phoebe said. "What do you say?"

Independence Rock looked like a large rock island jutting out of the flat landscape. The sun was setting as the Bentleys made their way to it. The sky shifted from blue to gold to pink to purple. It was a stunning sight, but the changing colors reminded Eliza of her lost lucky stone.

As her family approached the rock, Eliza gasped. There were so many names! Some were carved, others painted or written in coal. There were even some Indian symbols carved in the stone. Eliza ran her fingers over the symbols, wondering if they were names or messages and stories. She wished she could read them.

Robert was also running his fingers over the symbols, his eyes widened in wonder.

"Imagine being able to read any language," Robert said. "Every single person in the world has a story to tell. Wouldn't it be wonderful to hear them all?"

He pulled out his pocketknife and started carving his name into the rock. When he was finished, he handed the knife to Eliza.

"Let the world know you were here, my girl," Robert said.

After the entire family carved their names, they walked back to camp for a picnic. Many of the travelers were celebrating, singing patriotic songs.

Eliza pulled her father aside as her mother went to trade some of the family's butter for more supplies and Leander went to gather firewood.

"Father, can pacifists still celebrate Independence Day?" she asked.

"Of course," Robert said. "America is our home. And we are making progress toward something new and wonderful. I may not agree with all of the violence, but we live in a land that believes in the freedom of speech. We have much to be thankful for."

Leander came back with firewood and Robert helped him start the campfire. Eliza saw her mother making her way back, her arms full of supplies. Eliza ran off to help her, and the moment she removed the fabric and thread from her mother's arms, Phoebe turned away and vomited on the grass.

"Mother, what is wrong?" Eliza asked.

"Oh, it's nothing," Phoebe said, wiping

her mouth with a handkerchief. Despite her episode, her blonde hair stayed neatly tucked in her bonnet. "Just tired from the long day. I will be fine after a good night of rest."

Eliza wanted to shout at her mother for lying. She wanted to confront her about the illness. She wanted to hug her and never let go. But since her mother got sick the moment Eliza reached her, it was obvious to Eliza that the curse was to blame. She feared that touching her mother would make her even sicker. So she said nothing, just carried the supplies back to their campsite while keeping her distance from her mother.

When the family woke up the next morning to continue their journey, Eliza trailed behind, walking with Anti-Abigail. She was a bit afraid that her presence would cause the cow to produce spoiled milk or some other unlucky occurrence, but the cow's slow movement made it easier for her to keep her bad luck out of the range of her family.

"No offense, Anti-Abigail," Eliza said quietly as they walked. "But I can't risk my mother's safety."

The wretched cow had become her companion during those lonely days of travel. Every morning, after she rinsed the breakfast plates and mugs and stowed away the family's bedding, when one of the men would yell "Wagons ho!," to start the day's journey, Eliza would make her way to Anti-Abigail. She knew Leander missed her company, but she pretended she just wanted to do her part to help. She could tell Leander didn't believe her; still, he never argued.

But as the travelers reached Idaho and stopped for nooning, most everyone's favorite rest time, Leander ran up to his sister, a huge grin on his face.

"Father has been telling me all about Soda Springs," Leander said. "We should reach it in a day or two and it is supposed to be unlike anything we've ever seen!"

Eliza let Anti-Abigail wander off to graze as her brother spoke, but when the cow took a few steps across the muddy ground, she started to sink.

"Quicksand! Go get help," Eliza shouted to her brother. "Oh no, Anti-Abigail, don't thrash! Stay calm, girl."

Robert and some of the other men spent most of the day digging Anti-Abigail out of the muck. They lost half a day of travel, but the cow was saved. Eliza wanted to hug the poor animal, but feared the ground might just swallow them both up if she did.

Her guilt for bringing the curse was making Eliza very jumpy. It was impossible to stay away from everyone, so she had to settle for making sure she didn't touch anyone and no one touched her. So when her father put his hand on her shoulder or her mother reached for her hand, Eliza would wiggle away from the contact.

Still, when the family reached Soda Springs, Eliza was so amazed that she allowed Leander to grab her arm. With the mountains in the background, and the sun shining down on the water, it was one of the loveliest things she had ever seen.

"You haven't even seen the best part," Leander said, back to his habit of answering her unspoken thoughts. "Look at what the water does! Feel it!"

He pulled Eliza up to the springs, where they marveled at the bubbling water. When they dipped their hands in, they felt that the water was *warm!*

The warm, bubbling water delighted the travelers. It made that evening's laundry much easier. The women baked loaf after loaf of bread, as the warm water allowed them to prepare the dough without first preparing the water. And the water was wonderful to drink, the bubbles tickling their throats and making them giggle.

After so much bad luck, Soda Springs felt like a miracle to Eliza. She spent all afternoon near the springs, dancing and laughing with the other travelers.

"There is that funny daughter of mine," Robert said. "It has been weeks since a smile crossed your face. I was beginning to think we were traveling with the wrong girl."

"I have been troubled," Eliza said. "But I cannot tell you why without making it worse."

"Hmm," Robert said. "Well, help can come from unexpected places. I imagine the solution will turn up soon enough. Would you like to walk with me a bit? I am going to do some trading."

Though Eliza worried about his safety, she missed her father too much to refuse.

They walked beyond the boundaries of the campsite, her father nodding at the men who were setting up for their nightly guard shifts. After some time, they reached a small group of Indian men, including the two who saved Eliza from the wolf.

The younger one ran over to them and spoke to Robert.

"My father is ready for trade," the boy said.

"Wonderful! Eliza, you can stay here with Dichali," Robert said.

As her father walked over to trade supplies with the native men, Eliza turned to the boy.

"Dichali? Is that your name?" she asked.

"Yes," Dichali said. "It means 'speaks a lot.' My mother always said I was destined to learn many languages."

"Well, Dichali, I never got the chance to properly thank you," Eliza said. "You and your father saved me from becoming that wolf's dinner."

"I should thank you as well," Dichali said, smiling in a way that brightened his entire face. "If you had not wandered off, we may never have met your father. Trading with him has kept us alive. We were in dire need the night we met. After illness took my mother, my father decided to take off to the West. But we had a small traveling party and a lot of misfortune. Our luck changed the day we met."

"Really? Because my luck has gotten worse and worse," Eliza said.

Before she could stop herself, she told Dichali everything, all of her bad luck, her worries about her mother and the guilt that it could be all of her fault.

"Why would you think it is your fault?" he asked.

Eliza explained about the lucky stone, and she saw Dichali's eyes widen as she spoke.

She figured he thought she was crazy, but it felt so good to unburden herself, she kept speaking until the entire story unfurled.

"I can help you," he said.

Dichali reached into a leather pouch that hung around his waist. He withdrew his hand slowly, then opened his fist. The stone! He handed it to Eliza, who had trouble forming words.

"How? Wait, what? I mean… *how?*" she asked.

"I found it when we went to retrieve the wolf that night," Dichali said. "You must have just dropped it. And now it has found its way back to you."

Eliza felt a rush of gratitude like she had never known, followed by a quick pang of guilt.

"But if I take this, what if your bad luck returns?" she asked.

Dichali smiled again and Eliza thought it may have been the best smile she had ever seen.

"We have decided to stay here," Dichali said. "Have you been to those springs? How could bad luck possibly find its way to such a magical place?"

Robert came back, his arms full of furs, and reached out his hand to Dichali.

"Best of luck to you, young man," Robert said, shaking Dichali's hand. "I think you will make a very happy life here indeed."

As Eliza and her father walked back toward their camp, she turned and looked over her shoulder at Dichali and mouthed, "Thank you." She was rewarded with another captivating smile before he turned and made his way back to his father.

Chapter Six
NEW BEGINNING

For the first night in weeks, Eliza slept deeply without being interrupted by nightmares. She had tucked the lucky stone into her sleeping cap the night before, and the moment she woke up, she pulled off the cap and made sure it was still there. She clutched it to her chest, grinning widely. She felt her luck return, warm and wonderful. She was happily trying to tame her curls in her bonnet when she heard her mother retching outside.

Eliza ran outside, still in her nightgown. Her parents sat by the fire, preparing breakfast. The sun was not out yet, but Eliza could see her mother's queasy face by the firelight.

"How are you still sick?" Eliza asked, tears streaming down her face. "I broke the curse! I got the lucky stone back! Everything was supposed to get better! I won't let you die like Harriet's mother and Dichali's mother! I will run away first!"

Eliza ran over to Phoebe and buried her face in her mother's apron, knocking the bowl of cornmeal batter out of Phoebe's hands and onto the ground. The spilled Johnny Cake batter made Eliza cry even harder, her wails waking Leander. He emerged from the tent to see his sister sobbing on his mother's lap and his father wrapping his arms around both of them, trying to calm Eliza. Poe eagerly lapped up the batter, oblivious to the drama unfolding.

"What's going on?" Leander asked, rubbing his eyes.

"Mother is going to die because I am cursed," Eliza said, hiccupping through her tears. "So I have to run away and never see any of you ever again."

"What are you talking about, Eliza? I am not dying," Phoebe said.

"And what curse?" Robert asked.

Eliza took a deep breath and explained everything for the second time in two days. She clutched the stone in her fist, and as she finished her story, she opened her hand and showed it to her family.

"Against all odds, I got the stone back," Eliza said. "But Mother is still sick. So I must still be cursed."

"Eliza, I am not sick," Phoebe said. "I am with child."

"With child?" Leander asked.

"You're going to have a baby?" Eliza exclaimed.

Phoebe smiled at the twins and nodded. Robert kissed his wife on the forehead.

"We were going to wait to tell you until

we were settled in Oregon," Robert said. "Because we did not want you to worry about your mother and the new baby throughout the journey. We know how you worry, Eliza. And we knew Leander would never be able to keep such a secret from you."

Eliza felt relieved for a moment, then a troubled thought brought the nervous grasshoppers back to her stomach.

"But if I'm not cursed, then how come the batter spilled the moment I came out of the tent?" Eliza asked.

"Because you ran at your mother like a crazed bull, silly girl," Robert said. "That isn't a curse, it is just clumsiness."

The Bentleys started laughing, ignoring the strange looks from the other nearby travelers. They made quite a sight hugging and laughing like that, the twins still in pajamas, Eliza with her tear-stained face and wild hair loose in public, and Poe with his muzzle covered in Johnny Cake batter. They were certainly the most peculiar family on the campsite, but in that moment, they were also the happiest.

"Oh, and Eliza," Phoebe said. "Get into that tent and pull those curls into a bonnet, for goodness sake. You are a *lady*."

For the first time, Eliza smiled at her mother's command. Everything felt normal again.

During the following months, the Bentleys made it through Idaho as the temperature dropped and Phoebe's belly grew. They had good days and bad days, but no streak of bad luck. Though her parents insisted there was no such thing as a curse, Eliza kept the lucky stone safely tucked in her apron's pocket during the day, and under her sleeping cap at night.

The day the Bentleys crossed the border into Oregon, the weather was Eliza's favorite kind. There was an October chill in the air, but the sun was shining. When the travelers stopped to make camp for the evening, Eliza rushed through her chores so she'd have time to explore before the sun went down. She churned at top speed, singing loudly about how butter was overrated and biscuits tasted much better with jam. Even Anti-Abigail cooperated for once, allowing Eliza to milk her with minimal fuss.

When she was finished, she ran off to the top of Flagstaff Hill. Leander was already there, staring out into the Blue Mountains. She walked up next to him, admiring the majestic view. The twins both thought Oregon was the most gorgeous place they had ever seen.

"I have been thinking about the Stone of the Seven Skips," Eliza said, using the nickname her brother came up with for the lucky stone. "Based on where Lucy found it, the person who dropped it must have been traveling to Pittsburgh. Do you think the Great Fire would have happened if the stone was never lost?"

Eliza pulled the stone out of her apron pocket and rolled it between her palms.

"I think some things just happen," Leander said. "Terrible things, sometimes. But stone or no stone, magic is surely real. We just walked across the country! We made it to this stunning land, we are going to have a new brother or sister. We don't need a lucky stone to be the luckiest family in the world."

Just as Eliza was about to comment on her brother's surprising depth, Leander took the stone from her and examined it closely.

"I also think you think way too much," Leander said, chuckling.

The sun was setting over the mountains and the colorful sky made the world look like a lucky charm. Eliza put her arm around her brother.

"You may be right," she said, smiling. Then she snatched the stone out of his hand. "But we should probably hold onto this, anyway."

She ran back toward the family's campsite, Leander a step behind her. And when she tripped on a branch, causing Leander to win their unspoken race, she laughed and tried to brush off most of the dirt so her mother wouldn't go into early labor while scolding her.

Though she'd mostly let go of the idea the stone was responsible for her family's fate, before she got up, she checked her apron pocket to make sure it was still there.

Just in case.

About Western Expansion

Western Expansion began when United States President Thomas Jefferson bought the territory of Louisiana from France in 1803. The Louisiana Purchase made the United States twice as big and opened up new lands for Americans to explore. President Jefferson felt that expanding the country was important for its success, so he encouraged pioneers to travel out West. The Oregon Trail was a route that pioneers took to get across the country during Western Expansion. Travelers started following this path in the early 1800s. By 1843, "The Great Migration" had about 1,000 pioneers heading West in pursuit of a mysterious and promising new life. Independence, Missouri was a common starting point for travelers. Though there were a few variations in the route, many of the travelers visited the same landmarks, like Independence Rock and Soda Springs. In 1845, the idea of Manifest Destiny started gaining attention. Manifest Destiny was a belief that expanding America was God's will. On the Oregon Trail, Native Americans sometimes acted as guides and traded with pioneers. Several hundred pioneers and Native Americans killed one another during the journey, though most of the danger was due to disease caused by the hardships of travel. Cholera and dysentery were among the diseases that pioneers faced. Additional dangers included starvation, bad weather and animal attacks. Despite the dangers, traveling the Oregon Trail was a huge opportunity for pioneers. The West was a chance to start anew. Gold was eventually discovered in California in 1848, but even before then, pioneers were lured by the idea of new opportunities and fertile lands. Some of the pioneers simply wanted to escape from the expanding cities and changing landscape of the East.

Editor's note: The indigenous people of North America were referred to as Indians at the time this book takes place. The terms American Indian and Native American are now used instead.

Q & A
with Erin Palmer

1. What inspired you to write this book?

I love to travel and recently visited Oregon for the first time. I'm fascinated by the idea of embarking on a cross-country adventure to a new life.

2. What did you learn while doing your research?

It amazed me how resourceful the pioneers were. I have a hard time packing for a week-long vacation, but they had to bring their entire lives!

3. Why did you make the Bentleys "peculiar?"

I think that people who aren't afraid to be themselves are the most interesting people.

About the Author

Erin Palmer is a writer who loves to travel and read. Stories let people go anywhere and be anyone, and Erin is happy to spend her life creating those stories.

Websites to Visit

https://archive.org/details/msdos_Oregon_
Trail_The_1990

www.songsforteaching.com/themeunits/
pioneerstheme.htm

www.ducksters.com/history/westward_
expansion/oregon_trail.php

Writing Prompt

Travel drives this story forward. Write a story or poem about where you would go if you could travel anywhere in the world.